# Robin's Room

**Margaret Wise Brown**

paintings by

**Steve Johnson and Lou Fancher**

Hyperion Books for Children
New York

When he was a little boy, he left his things all over the house.

He hollered when he woke up in the morning.

He left a **sneaker** full of sand in his mother's bed.

He took the toy mice away from the cat and tied them to chairs.

He hid things under the rug.

He painted **pictures** on the doors and windows.

He sawed legs off of chairs.

And he planted flowers in the bathtub.

"What will we ever do with this child?" his parents cried.

"He is underfoot, overhead, in our hair, and all over the place."

"Keep him on a leash," said the dog.

"Give him a room of his own," said the cat.

So when he wasn't a baby anymore, when he was the boy Robin,

his parents took him to a new door and said,

"In there is your own room."

Robin opened the door and there was his room.

"How do you like it?" they asked.

"Ouch!" said Robin.

"Don't you like it?" they asked.

"No," said Robin, "I don't,"
and he **stamped** his foot so hard that his shoe fell off.

Their mouths fell open. "What now? What next?" they said.

"Give me three carpenters, please," said Robin.

"What for?" they asked.

"For turning the fronts of everything to the back," said Robin.

His parents looked at him and then at each other.

"Why not?" said his father.

"Why not?" said his mother. "A child's room made by a child."

So they hired Robin three carpenters

and got him all he needed to fix up the room for himself.

For one week no one was allowed in that room
but Robin and the three carpenters.

On the other side of the door they could hear
hammering and splashing and tearing wood
and little **thuds.**

"What kind of a room is that child making for himself?"
everyone wondered.

Robin didn't tell.

But inside the room this is what he was doing.

On one wall he hung a **strip of cork.**

That was to pin things on.

And to unpin things as he changed them—

all sorts of things—butterflies and beetles,

postcards, stamps, labels, colored papers,

pictures, his own drawings, anything, **anything**—

On that cork wall, these things would come and go.

And he had two barrels:

one to throw things away in,

and one to keep things in.

He painted pictures on his barrels.

And he had a **closet.**

And he painted pictures
on his closet door,
which was like an easel,
with a shelf for jars of
paint and water and brushes
that couldn't spill when
the closet door swung open.

And Robin had a workbench built for himself.

A long heavy wooden workbench.

This was his table and his desk and his carpenter's bench.

And he had a **wonderful wide** window that he could sit in.

There was a place for flowers to grow beside him so that they bloomed right under his nose. He didn't have to lean over to smell them.

And he planted a tree in a wooden tub in one corner of the room.

In the spring he hung cherries on his tree.

In the summer roses,

in the autumn nuts,

and in the winter bananas.

And his bed was a wonderful bed to behold.

"You can reach everything from your bed," said his uncle. "Why get up?"

"Why not?" said Robin.

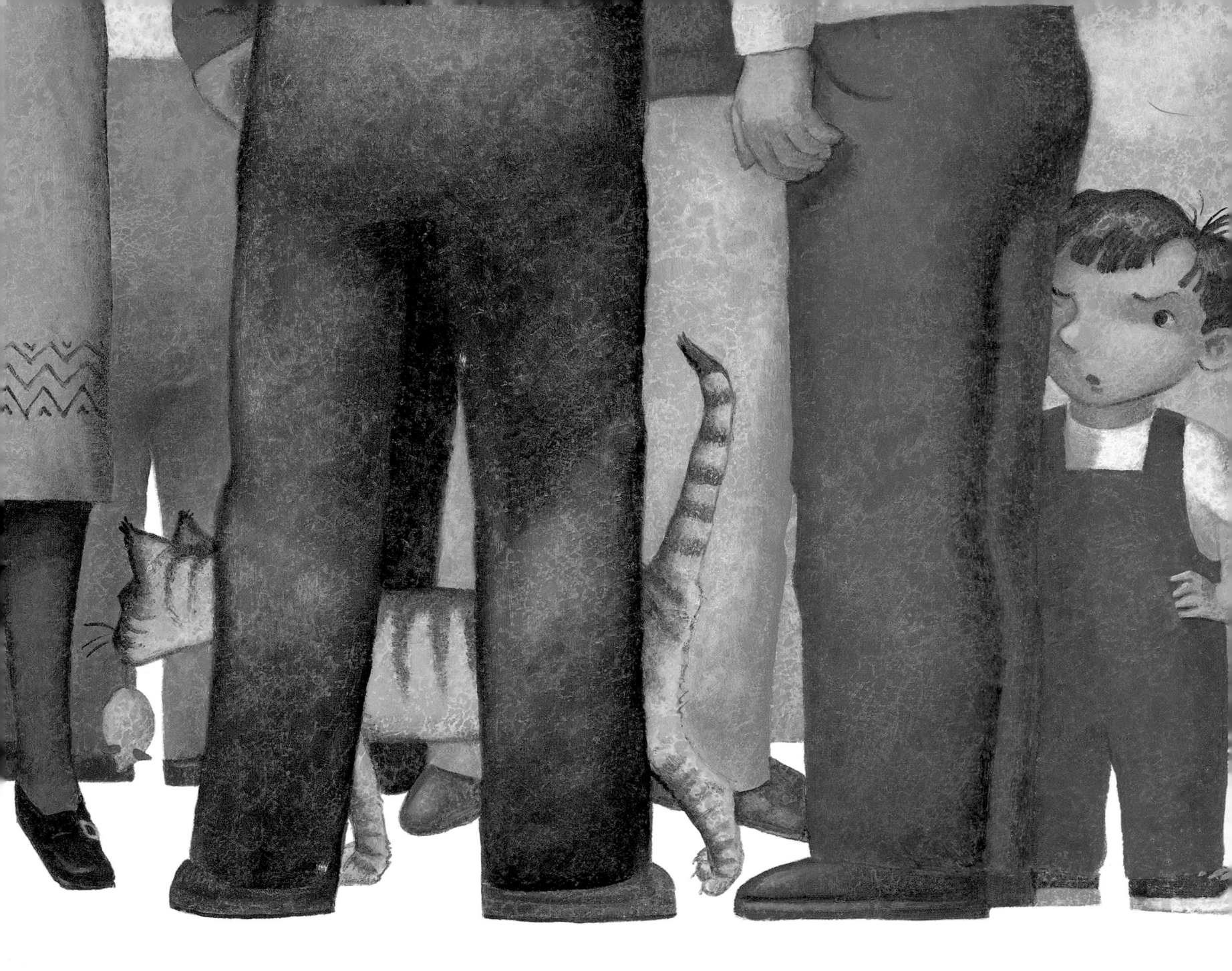

And his father brought their friends up to say **good** night.

And the dog brought his bone up.

And the cat brought his mouse up.

Everyone came to see his room.

And when they saw it they said it was the best room in the house.

And his mother came up to sit in the window and read.

enormous clock. And over the numbers he had painted pictures of his day. From four o'clock to suppertime he cut out a **space**. That was when he

"This clock," said Robin, for he had made an

"What clock?" they asked.

when my clock says they can't."

And everyone can come up to my room except

This is not the whole house. This is my own room.

But Robin said, "Oh, no you don't,

could do whatever he wanted to do all by himself alone in his room.

And from then on, Robin did not leave his things all over the house.

He did not holler when he woke up in the morning.

He did not leave a sneaker full of sand in his mother's bed.

He **did not** tie mice to chairs.

He did not hide anything under the rug, or paint pictures on windows,

or saw off chair legs, or plant flowers in the bathtub.

He had a room of his own.

For Max—
    *S. J. and L. F.*

Designed by Lou Fancher

First Edition
1 3 5 7 9 10 8 6 4 2

Printed in Singapore

Library of Congress Cataloging-in-Publication Data on file
ISBN 0-7868-0602-8 (hc)
ISBN 0-7868-2516-2 (lib. ed.)

Visit www.hyperionchildrensbooks.com

the end!